The Dreams of Youth

Stories by

L INDA M AHKOVEC

Other Books by Linda Mahkovec

Seven Tales of Love

The Garden House

The Christmastime Series

Christmastime 1940: A Love Story

Christmastime 1941: A Love Story

Christmastime 1942: A Love Story

Christmastime 1943: A Love Story

For my mother,
Agnes Mandeville Mahkovtz

Stages of Life

A Girl's Will

A [girl's] will is the wind's will. —Longfellow

December, 1925. Maggie was born in rural Illinois on the shortest day of the year.

"That's why you're so short," they used to tease her.

She thought it was remarkable that she was born on such a special day, and kept the thought of it tucked away like a treasure. Despite being shaped by the Great Depression and raised without a mother, Maggie radiated delight in the world around her. Daring and determined, she kept up with her older siblings and was protective of the younger ones. When her brothers and sisters staged a circus in the back yard for the entertainment of the neighborhood, it was eight-year-old Maggie who flew through the air on the handmade trapeze, her sense of adventure overriding any fear she might have had.

"One penny to see the Flying Wonder – Maggie!" they cried, drawing a sizable crowd.

Maggie loved the feeling of flying through the air and landing on the old mattress – the freedom, the thrill! It was the same feeling she had when she jumped from the hayloft onto the hay below, the same feeling she had when she rode her brother's bike and coasted with her arms outstretched.

Maggie was four when her mother Eileen died after giving birth to twins, the last of ten children. Eileen's body was laid out in the parlor. Narrow shafts of sunlight shone through the pulled curtains and mixed with the yellow glow from the lamps, creating for Maggie a confusing sense of it being neither day nor night. The cruelty of the tragedy was softened by the Irish keening and soft weeping of the relatives, and the murmuring concerns of the priests and nuns.

"What will they do?"

"Oh, the poor, poor children."

"He can't take care of them. They stand to lose the farm as it is."

Maggie's father stood silent, stunned.

Among the mourners, two black-clad factions took shape. The palpable anger of one side threatened to break through the wounded defense of the other. One side wanted to blame, the other to protect. For the doctor had warned Eileen against another pregnancy. Yet no amount of recrimination or stony stares could have increased the guilt and sorrow in Maggie's father. The shadow of grief was never to leave his face. For fifty more years he was haunted by his wife's beauty and love, and blamed himself for the loss that defined his life and the lives of his children. The thought of remarrying never entered his mind.

Maggie gazed on her beautiful sleeping mother and wanted only one thing – to be next to her. It had been days with no goodnight kiss, no one to add raisins to her oatmeal, no one to listen to her tales of the day. She began to climb into the coffin, and threw a tantrum when they pulled her away. She almost made it in the second time, and had one leg over the side. With tears on her cheeks and fierce determination in her eyes, she hid behind the potted fern in the corner. She would wait for them all to go away. Then she would climb in and once more rest in the arms of her mother.

Hours later, they found her curled up in the corner, and carried her up to bed.

For days and weeks she wandered around the house, looking for her mother, listening for her voice.

*

Summers at home were magical. The rest of the year was spent in the orphanage, along with the twins and her sisters. Maggie came to love the nuns. They taught her how to sew and read, and told wondrous stories about the lives of the saints.

All the same, she was happy when she finally reached high school and moved back home. By then, the family had moved to town. Maggie found jobs working at the hospital switchboard, and babysitting after school and on weekends. She was saving up for the time when she would venture forth into the wide world. Her two sisters decided to become nuns, but Maggie knew that another future awaited her. She could see it, feel it. Looking out her bedroom window into the sun-dappled treetops, she imagined the glittering ocean, faraway cities, adventure, romance.

Maggie had long wanted to be a nurse. She liked helping people, and she wanted to be able to support herself. When she learned that airline stewardesses were required to be registered nurses, a plan began to blossom. She loved the idea of planes, and flying, and travel. Here was a way for her to help others – and see the world. So she signed up for the Cadet Program, which paid for her tuition. By the time her sisters were novices and her brothers were in the seminary or the military, Maggie was getting her nurse's pin.

She took her savings and journeyed by bus to Kansas City for an interview with TWA. Her dreams were finally going to come true; she could feel them tingling at her fingertips. From the bus window, she imagined the miles and miles of corn as the wideness of the ocean, curving into the horizon. The golden wheat became the golden sand where she would soon stand and let the waves lap over her bare feet. When she closed her eyes, she could almost feel the salt spray on her face!

As she waited in a long line with other hopefuls, eager for the interview, she heard the whispers.

"They don't hire girls with glasses. You must have perfect vision."

Maggie took off her glasses and slipped them into her pocket. Her dreams began to shrink and hide. During a game of tag one summer, Maggie's brother had swung a weeping willow branch that caught her in the eye. The interview included a vision test. The gentlemen thanked her for coming, and said they would contact her if they were interested.

Back home, Maggie found a job working in the veteran's hospital, along with several of her friends from nursing school. The hospital was full of wounded soldiers home from the battlefields of Europe and the Pacific, and the need for nurses was great. What Maggie most remembered from this period in her life were the dying soldiers; they never wanted to die at night. Maggie sat with them and held their hands as they tried to hold on until the first glimmer of dawn. The longing and yearning in those sad, young men was to stay with her forever.

Maggie had not given up on her dreams of seeing the world. While she was working at the

VA hospital, she learned that her vision was good enough to enlist in the Air Force Nurse Corps. She would become a military flight nurse.

But that plan would have to wait, for Maggie was handed a different key to her future.

"There's loads of work out there! And we can stay with my aunt until we find a place of our own."

When Maggie's best friend from nursing school offered her the chance to go to California – the land of dreams – Maggie knew that the door to her future had opened at last.

The B-Movie Actress

There are things of which I may not speak; / There are dreams that cannot die. —Longfellow

The graduating nursing class of '47 was held at St. Mary's Church. Dressed in crisp white uniforms and caps, and dark blue capes, sixteen eager young women awaited their nurses' pins. Two women stood out from the rest – Rita and Maggie, who, from day one, had recognized a kindred spirit in each other. As with all the graduates, they were proud of their accomplishment, but a different light shone out from their faces – a suppressed excitement surfacing from the dreams that were connected to their graduation. Maggie, with a far-away ardent look, was going to save the world. Rita, more fiery and ambitious, was going to dazzle the world.

The two girls had both lost their mothers at an early age, which perhaps accounted for their willingness to leave the Midwest. The other nurses didn't want to be far from home, but Rita and Maggie had a sense of adventure and were far more daring in their dreaming. They were going to get out of the Midwest and see the world.

Rita's plan was to support herself by nursing so that she could study acting and become a movie star. When she asked Maggie to move with her to Los Angeles, Maggie didn't have to think twice. They would finally get to see the ocean, and be a part of the Hollywood glamour that had nourished their small-town dreams, and live life on a grander scale.

Rita and Maggie packed their bags, took the train north to Chicago, and then transferred to the Pacific line that headed to the Golden State. On the train they traded their favorite poems from high school, with Rita performing dramatic readings of them. They were not surprised to discover that they both loved "A Psalm of Life," "My Lost Youth," "Annabel Lee," and "Invictus." The friends had similar mottos and were prepared to live by them: Rita's was "Carpe diem," Maggie's was "Find the beauty in the day."

The two young women caught the attention of people from Chicago to Los Angeles, and all stops in between. Both beauties, their Irish blood gave them a similar appearance: slender figures, curly black hair, green eyes. But where Maggie had a softness about her, Rita had a feistiness that she claimed came from her mix.

"I'm a spick and a mick," she proudly joked, and the fire in her eyes challenged anyone to make what they would of that.

Their Catholic school upbringing gave them an air of propriety that strained to contain their irrepressible liveliness. At one moment they appeared all decorous and demure, while the next, they doubled over in helpless, tear-streaming laughter.

They stayed for a month with Rita's aunt, and found jobs within the first week. They then roomed with two other nurses who worked at the same hospital.

Rita signed up for acting classes two weeks later, confident that she had the right combination of qualities that would allow her to succeed in film. She quickly took on the glamour of an actress, much of which rubbed off on Maggie. They wore the classic red lipstick of the day, kept their hair in short curls, and wore sundresses and sandals in the day, stylish evening dresses and heels at night.

Rita always had handsome young men begging to do her small favors. Once, she allowed her beau of the day to drive her and Maggie to Yosemite, and then pick them up three days later. The girls stayed at a small rented cabin and had the time of their lives hiking in the beautiful park. The ever-daring Maggie would fearlessly stand near the edge of a cliff or atop a tall rock while Rita photographed her. Now and then, an obliging hiker would snap the two of them, wearing their checked shirts, rolled-up jeans, saddle shoes – and red lipstick.

They saw as many radio and stage plays as possible, and small adventures never failed to enter into their outings. One night, they met Jimmy Durante outside The Brown Derby, and he gave them front-row tickets to *The Andrew Sisters Radio Show*. They laughed till they cried, and sang their songs for weeks.

Then there was the evening after watching *South Pacific*. They stopped at a nearby café, took their seats at a long counter, and discussed the lively production.

Rita suddenly became excited when she saw the man two stools down. She nudged Maggie. "That's Burt Lancaster!" she whispered. "Say something!"

Maggie knew she would never forgive herself if she didn't speak. So even though they were just having coffee, she bravely turned to him.

"Excuse me. Can you please pass the salt?" she asked.

He looked at her cup of coffee, and then handed her the salt, watching to see what she would do with it.

Feeling his eyes on her, Maggie shook some salt into her coffee and passed it to Rita, who did the same. When he didn't look away, they had no choice but to drink the coffee.

He slowly shook his head and went back to reading the paper.

The two women assumed an elegant, sophisticated demeanor as they sipped their salty coffee, their shoulders only slightly shaking from their suppressed laughter.

However, the ways of Hollywood were sorely at odds with their Midwestern, Catholic upbringing. After a year, Maggie found the pace of Los Angeles too trying and moved north to the smaller seaside town of Santa Barbara.

Rita often visited her there and the two spent their time picnicking on the beach, sitting at outdoor cafés, and strolling through the pretty town in their sundresses and straw hats. Rita always updated Maggie on her glamorous life as an actress. She studied acting for a few years and through sheer determination, made it into a few B movies, Westerns mostly.

Maggie never missed any of her movies, and when Rita's scene filled the screen, Maggie leaned to the person next to her, and whispered, "That's my friend, Rita. Isn't she wonderful?"

But after several trying years, Rita became worn down by an industry that was interested only in her physical attributes. She grew tired of the crude advances, tired of being asked how she was in the hay, tired of being dismissed when she gave a smart answer. After one too many assaults on her dignity, she moved back to the Midwest. But after an abusive first marriage and a demanding second one, Rita wondered what the difference was, and thought she might as well have given herself bodily to a career as to marriage.

*

Rita often thought of her friend Maggie, who was quieter and more attached to the vocation of nursing than she had ever been. Perhaps, thought Rita, I have reached too high. Perhaps I should have been more like Maggie, seeking out the simple beauties of the day. That's where the real romance of life was to be found, Maggie used to say. That happiness was not found in a man, or in a career, or in any one thing, but in the tiny connections to beauty and meaning woven into the day.

It sounded so simple. It came effortlessly to Maggie – she found it in the color of the sky, the scent of a flower, the laughter of children. But the only beauty and meaning Rita had ever found came from struggling through the briars and brambles of life, a search that left her lashed and bleeding.

In Santa Barbara, Maggie joined the Air Force Nurse Corps, still determined to become a flight nurse. Because of her years of experience as a nurse, she was made First Lieutenant, and was sent back to her home state of Illinois to complete her training.

Rita was disappointed to hear that Maggie met a man while she was there and became engaged, and that she later married him and settled down in rural Illinois. Rita had always planned on visiting Maggie in California, and had thought that as long as Maggie was living there, then her dreams, too, were still alive.

Rita's fire and beauty enabled her to overcome the stigma that would otherwise have been attached to a twice-divorced woman. And it was determination, rather than love, that resulted in a third successful marriage, this time to a kindlier man.

She moved with him to Chicago and settled into relative happiness. The demands of raising children and caring for a home and husband absorbed much of her fire. And at the end of the day, she slept peacefully enough, only now and then starting from a dream of stage lights illuminating her performance, or a camera angled on her profile. Then for a few days, her old fire would flare, only to then sputter in frustration. Those close to her knew to keep their distance.

However, Rita was not yet through with her dreams. This third marriage had given her two children, and one was a daughter. *She* would be an actress.

*

As the years went by, Rita and Maggie were consumed by their busy lives. They kept in touch with letters and phone calls, and cards at Christmastime. Rita always included a professional Christmas photograph of her family, and as she posted the card to her old friend, a feeling of gratification coursed through her. The photo was proof of her successful life, proof that she hadn't changed. There was the same dazzling smile, the crisp, fashionable style. The only difference was that now she was surrounded by her adoring husband and children.

One Saturday, she took the train with her two children from Chicago down to the small town where Maggie lived. Rita proudly registered the delight in Maggie's eyes at finding her old friend remarkably the same: trim, spirited, elegant.

Maggie by then had five children. Rita was almost affronted by Maggie's effortless beauty and happiness, and while Maggie recounted Rita's success in the movies to the wide-eyed children, Rita openly flirted with Maggie's husband, putting her cheek next to his for the photographs, letting her hand linger too long on his arm. He clearly enjoyed the attention, and Rita imagined what an easy conquest he would be. For a moment, she felt pity for the smiling, generous Maggie.

But then she stiffened in indignant rage when she realized that Maggie saw through her act – saw that she, the beautiful glamorous Rita, needed the spotlight now more than ever. Rita recognized the same selfish desperation in Maggie's husband, and knew that he, too, derived a tiny pleasure in hurting Maggie, who was so complete in herself, who never struggled with the self-doubts and anger of unrealized dreams.

As Rita dramatically waved goodbye from the train, she realized how happy Maggie had been to see her. Her own feelings at seeing her friend were more complicated and conflicted. And yet she felt a gripping sadness as she watched her friend recede in the distance.

Rather than let her tears fall, she snapped at her children to sit up straight.

*

Eventually, their communication dwindled down to just the cards at Christmas. Rita's life was increasingly busy with auditions for her daughter, and entertaining at home for her husband's career. Maggie was busy raising five children and dealing with the struggles of a small town economy and an increasingly alcoholic husband. The years went by and the friends grew older as they tried to make the best of their lives.

Rita burned with anger when she was told she had advanced cancer. She was angry that she wouldn't get to see her daughter succeed where she had not. Angry at the people who had hurt her in life. Angry that her grand dreams had come to so little.

She didn't tell Maggie that she was dying. Let her find out for herself, she thought bitterly.

But in the end, it was the memory of Maggie and their time in California that got her through the hardest periods. On the days when she could speak, she relived those years by recounting their stories to her children. She lavished praise on Maggie for her humor, her gentleness, her convictions.

On the days when her voice failed her, she had her children read the poems she and Maggie had so loved. Rita alternated between smiles and tears as her daughter read the lines from "My Lost Youth":

And with joy that is almost pain
My heart goes back to wander there,
And among the dreams of the days that were,
I find my lost youth again.

And Rita silently cursed the pride and stubbornness that prevented her from seeing her old friend, one last time.

My Princess

Often I think of the beautiful town / That is seated by the sea. —Longfellow

Maggie looked out the kitchen window as she washed the dishes from supper. This was the first set; there would be another when Frank came home from the tavern. She was glad their eldest daughter was gone for the evening; that would be one less argument, in case he came home in a quarrelsome mood. She would just have to pray that he wouldn't get into it with their teenage son, who was listening to music in his bedroom.

Maggie never knew if a happy husband would walk through the door, or an unhappy, difficult husband. Most likely, it would be a combination of both, alternating unpredictably. A knot formed in her stomach, as it did in the three children watching television in the family room, when she heard his truck pull in the driveway.

Maggie took his dinner from the oven, placed it on the table, and breathed a sigh of relief. It was a happy husband who came in the door. She heard him laughing as he briefly wrestled with their two young sons. Then, while he took off his shoes, he asked their younger daughter what she learned in school that day. He stood up and wove his way into the kitchen, followed by the children. They sat at the table with him, hungry for his attention.

Frank's eyes focused unsteadily on the food before him. He laughed to himself, and then out loud, at some story that lingered in his mind from the tavern. He rambled a bit as he tried to relate the story to his kids, but when it didn't come out right, he gave it up.

Instead, he shifted to his routine storytelling. He rubbed the whiskers on his cheek, making a rough scratching sound, and rummaged around in his mind for a familiar theme. His sons hoped he would settle on a war story, and groaned when they heard the mushy preamble to the oft-told story.

"Did I ever tell you who my princess was?"

The boys got up and went back to *Gunsmoke*. The daughter listened respectfully, hoping his mood would last until he fell asleep on the living room floor.

Maggie looked out the window, farther into the darkness, searching for a vision from long ago that might sustain her through the evening. It was usually a vision of the seaside town she had lived in during her younger days in California. Perhaps the happiest she had ever been, when everything was before her. She remembered the countless strolls through the town, the little boutique where she had bought her favorite dress, the hospital where the patients loved her, the café where she first tasted an avocado, the golden sand, those magnificent sunsets.

"Your mother. My Maggie. That's my *princess*. My best friend and my *princess*." He emphasized the word when he came to it, weighting it with imagined significance.

He slurred as he spoke, though he deftly picked at the chicken, putting the bare bones in a neat little pile on his plate. His favorite part of the baked chicken was the bony back, which he referred to as the carcass. That's where all the nutrients were, he always claimed. Maggie knew that this preference came from the lean Depression days of his youth – along with his love of blood sausage and head cheese, his insistence every summer on canning tomatoes and beans from the garden, and his habit of adding water to the empty ketchup bottle, so as not to waste any.

Maggie caught some of his familiar refrains and wove them into her vision outside the dark window, as she soaped and rinsed the dishes.

"I first saw your mom, my *princess*, at a wedding. She was the prettiest girl I ever saw. I knew I was going to marry her."

Maggie acknowledged to herself that she had been equally attracted to Frank, the handsome tail gunner she had met in St. Louis while he was attending college and she was working at the Red Cross. They were soon inseparable, going to stage plays and parties and picnics.

She had been ready to settle down, Maggie always claimed. Ready to have a family. No regrets. While other women complained of the cooking and cleaning, the mounds of ironing, scrubbing floors, and washing of diapers, she had accepted it as part of the territory of motherhood. She took pure delight in anything to do with their children.

And Frank was fun back then. Maggie didn't know how much of his downward spiral was caused by the lingering effects of the war, and how much was caused by the simple wear and tear of life.

No regrets, and yet they were there.

She thought of her friend Rita, and wondered why they had lost touch. She blamed Frank for those terrible years, years that prevented her from thinking of anything but survival – his violent arguments with the kids, his betrayals, her attempt to work as a nurse again and his rage against it, her humiliation when he forced her to give it up.

She kept to herself those years, and avoided reaching out to Rita or to anyone else. But the consequence of her withdrawal came crashing down on her when she received the phone call from Rita's daughter, saying that her mother had died. Maggie's regret that she hadn't sought out Rita filled her with a sadness that she had only slowly learned to live with.

As she dried the dishes, dark despair began to swell and rise inside her. She forced it down, telling herself, "The good times, remember the good times."

"My *princess!*" laughed Frank. "I couldn't wait to get into her pants."

Maggie realized that Frank's rambling had taken a turn, and she told him to stop talking that way and to eat his supper.

He pushed his plate away. "I can't eat this! It's all dried out. Tastes like leather."

Maggie responded futilely, "If you would come home when you're supposed to, it wouldn't be so dry." Futile, because she knew he wouldn't remember anything the next day, when the pattern would repeat itself.

His tone suddenly changed to spiteful. "And where's that daughter of yours?"

Nothing made Maggie angrier than when he referred to their children as hers, implying that they weren't his. That was *his* way, not hers. She hid the knowledge of his affairs from the children, afraid of how they would react.

"On the road like horse shit!" he slurred.

Maggie recognized that his mood had shifted, and that he was ready to pick a fight. She avoided that at all costs. "She's studying with a friend."

Frank first laughed at the idea, and then became disgusted. "She's out again with that long-haired good-for-nothing. Just like her mother, always on the road…" Now came the attack on her, his princess.

Their eldest son came out to the kitchen, ready to defend his mother. Things could get dangerous. Maggie knew she had to stop Frank's ranting before the name-calling started, for then her son couldn't control himself.

"Come on, Frank," she said, helping him to his feet. "Go lie down, while I clean up the dishes."

Maggie steered him in the direction of the living room. Frank stumbled into the room, and then sprawled out in the middle of the carpet. Soon his muttering was replaced by loud snores.

Their son said he was going out for a while with his friends.

Maggie cleared the table and finished the dishes. She gazed out the window again as she washed his plate, but the black night held no more visions.

Maggie looked down at her rough red hands, and then up at her reflection. She positioned herself slightly to the left, so that the wreath on the wall behind her formed a sort of crown around her head, princess-like.

The Finnish Boy

And the thoughts of youth, are long, long thoughts.
—Longfellow

Maggie took a stroll around her front garden at the end of day. A light breeze ruffled her nearly-white hair and caused the first leaves of autumn to scatter around her. She pulled her sweater close as she looked up at the billowy clouds in the western sky. It promised to be a beautiful sunset.

Across the way, a car pulled in the driveway and Maggie saw that her neighbor's father, Harry, was over for a visit. A fellow veteran like herself, Maggie always saluted him whenever she saw him.

Maggie watched him struggle out of the car, and as he looked over, she snapped him a salute.

Harry raised his hand to his forehead and stood a little straighter. He chuckled as he walked into the house, arm in arm with his daughter, his oxygen tank trailing behind him.

Maggie remembered with a smile how Frank had always been both proud and amused that, militarily, she outranked him. She briefly wondered what Frank would be like now, had he lived longer. The response came immediately: crotchety and difficult, only older. Ah well, there had been good times, along with the bad. And despite everything, the love had always been there.

Maggie looked at her roses, and pulled off a few faded petals. She inhaled their fragrance and exhaled an audible sigh of delight. She got a good grip on the railing before climbing the three steps to the porch. Before she sat on the bench, she tapped the wind chimes to make them ring.

There was a beauty about her still; the lines on her face were made mostly from laughing and smiling. Only now and then did a wistful look cross her face, caused by the unexpected stirring of memories, and certain regrets that eighty-five years of living were sure to produce.

Some regrets were vague, but others came from specific memories still fresh in her mind, as if they had just occurred. Such as the one that stirred now, as the light of day began to soften and fade. It was a memory that gave her a pang of regret each time it surfaced, and that the years since had done nothing to diminish. An incident that happened in 1949, when she was a young nurse in Santa Barbara, in California.

California! The name still held the same magic as it did when she was young, when the first dreams of leaving her small town began to form. For a young girl in Depression-era Illinois, California held everything that was bright and beautiful, exciting and promising. Maggie had a zest to see the world, to have adventures, to stretch her wings and see what she could do. Becoming a nurse had been the best way out of the Midwest and into her dreams.

Maggie had made her way to Santa Barbara, a town so like the picture postcards she had seen as a girl. One of those pretty, coastal towns with red-tiled roofs and palm trees and a blue, blue sky. She had dreamed of the ocean ever since she was a girl, imagined standing in the surf with the salt spray on her face.

The ocean never ceased calling to her, even after she returned to the rural Midwest. Frank wasn't much of a traveler, so it was long years before she saw California again, after their eldest son had moved out there. She imagined herself now, standing in the same shimmering surf, with bony feet and a slight bend in her back. *My ocean*, she always called it.

In Santa Barbara, Maggie lived alone in a pretty stucco apartment building with a small fountain in the courtyard. Flowers bloomed year round, which never ceased to amaze her – pink roses, orange poppies, and exotic flowers that reached up from spiky succulent plants. The palm trees never lost their leaves, like Midwestern trees. Their green fronds glistened eternal-like in the ever-present sun.

Maggie walked to and from the hospital dressed in her crisp white uniform and cap. She worked the 3:00 – 11:00 p.m. shift and was responsible for twenty-nine beds on her floor. She loved her work, the sense of purpose it gave her, of being able to make a difference in the lives of others. She had friends who preferred to work in Los Angeles, but Santa Barbara suited Maggie perfectly. It was exciting, but on a smaller, more charming scale.

One night, at around 7:00, a nurse and an orderly brought a patient from the Emergency Room to Maggie's floor. The ER nurse explained that the young man had been in a bad road accident. The doctors had done what they could, but after working on him for two hours, they shook their heads, hooked him up to a morphine drip, and sent him to Maggie's floor. The nurse said that he had been muttering in a foreign language that no one recognized. She handed Maggie the report and left.

Maggie saw that the patient was just a boy, around twenty-four years old or so, her own age. He was tall and slim, with fair hair and a handsome face. As she gazed down on him, his blue eyes opened and fixed on her.

Maggie smiled her nurse's smile, competent and compassionate. By then, the morphine had worked its magic, and he didn't seem to be in too much pain. He watched her as she adjusted his pillow and blanket, his eyes searching her face for an answer.

As she took his pulse, he turned his wrist and clasped her hand. Maggie spoke a few gentle words of comfort and was surprised when he answered in English. He thanked her and asked her name. He told her he was from Finland. That he had wanted to see the United States and had found work driving trucks for a transport company. He smiled when he said it was the best way to see such a big country. He soon became fatigued and closed his eyes.

Maggie was concerned about her other patients, but each time she tried to leave, he opened his eyes and tightened the hold on her hand.

When Maggie told him that she had to check on her patients, he became agitated and a look of fear filled his eyes. He said he didn't want to be alone. Maggie smiled and promised him she would be right back.

She went out and spoke briefly to the other nurse on duty and explained that she needed to sit with the new patient. The nurse assured her that the other patients were either resting quietly or sleeping, and that she would answer any calls or lights.

Maggie was thankful that the night was slow. She couldn't leave him alone. There was no hope for him, and she guessed that he knew. She took a deep breath and returned to his bedside.

The sun was beginning to set and the room was slowly growing darker. She turned on the nightlight above his bed. As soon as she sat down, he opened his hand for hers. It seemed that he wanted to talk.

Maggie asked him which parts of the States he had seen. He became slightly more animated as he described the Great Plains, the Rocky Mountains, and the Northwest. But when he described the coast of California, a softer look filled his face. He told her it was the most beautiful place he had ever seen. Maggie replied that she felt the same way, and that she, too, had come from far away to be near the beautiful California coast.

She then asked him about the place he was from. In a few spare words, he told her that he was from a small town, a small family. He said he had wanted to see the world. His voice quivered slightly when he told her how his family had taken him to the train station – how his mother had cried, how his father had tried hard not to cry, and how his younger brother and sister had run alongside the train until he couldn't see them anymore.

He was quiet for a few moments, and his mind seemed to shift. Then he told her about the accident. He said he had been driving, enjoying the beautiful scenery along the coast, and that all of a sudden someone from the oncoming lane passed a car and was in his lane. He said he knew that if he hit the car, the driver would be killed. And he couldn't do that. So he turned the wheel, and went over the hill. The next thing he remembered was the sound of a siren in his mind that grew louder and louder.

He looked at Maggie and told her that he didn't want to die. He didn't want to die so far from home. Somehow, he knew. And there was nothing Maggie could do but try to comfort him. She held his hand and tried to look strong, though she felt a sad crumbling inside her. Then she leaned closer and put her other hand on his cheek. This gesture of tenderness seemed to ease his anxiety, and his eyes glittered with gratitude. It was becoming more difficult for him to speak. He asked Maggie to tell him about her, where she was from.

She told him about her family, about how she was from a small town in the rural Midwest. How she became a nurse so that she could see something of the world, and how the ocean had always called to her.

They smiled, realizing how similar they were in their youthful dreams. His eyes fastened on her as he drank in her words, eager to take in just a little bit more of life. His speech trickled down to a few words, uttered slowly now and then. After a little while, he closed his eyes.

Maggie continued to speak in a soft, low voice, watching his face closely. She gently began to move away, thinking that he had fallen unconscious, but he increased the pressure on her hand. So she continued to sit with him, lightly squeezing his fingers to let him know that she was there.

Then she covered his hand with both of hers and sat quietly. And even though she was expecting it, she started when his hand went limp. She looked closely at his face, his chest, and leaned in to feel for a pulse. Her fingers searched again and again, but his warm wrist no longer held life. She placed her ear to his chest, but heard only silence. She watched him for a few moments, and put her hand to his cheek once more. Then she swallowed her emotions, and left the room.

Maggie stayed late that night to finish her reports. She walked home slowly, not noticing the tears on her cheeks. She made her way to the beach and stood for a few minutes, looking out at the glittering dark ocean, the wind blowing her hair.

*

Maggie shifted on her bench, and sorrow filled her face as she remembered that long-ago day. She often thought how strange it was, that there they were – two young people from such different parts of the world, that chance had brought together for a few hours in a hospital room in California. Both so far from home. Two young people who just wanted to see the world, to take all their hopes and dreams from their small towns and go forth, to live! She imagined that just as she was getting her nurse's pin and planning to leave her town, the Finnish boy was boarding the train, waving goodbye to his family.

Maggie remembered the many times she had thought of him throughout her life. At odd moments, the memory of him would suddenly surface, as vivid as if it had just happened, though long years had passed. She might have been doing dishes as she looked out the kitchen window, or holding the hand of one of her sick children, or burning the trash on a snowy day – and there he would be. His blue eyes searching hers, his face a mixture of sadness and homesickness and fear and gratitude, his hand using up its last bit of strength to cling to hers.

She often wondered if a part of her didn't die that night, along with the Finnish boy. The part that is made up of youthful dreams, of hope and long-ing. She often wondered if his death had anything to do with the fact that within a year, she was back in the Midwest, engaged to a Midwestern boy, near her family, and soon to be starting one of her own.

What she didn't know then was how strong those dreams of youth were, how relentlessly they continued to tug at her all her life. The pull of the ocean, the beauty of seaside towns, the promise of the world opening up to her – those longings never left her.

Maggie looked out at the fading day. The slanting rays of the sun cast the garden in a soft golden light and deepened the shadows. As the sun slowly sank, it created a rosy sky in the west that gradually faded to gray. And there it was – the pang of regret that hit her as it always did, the regret that had pulled at her for years: that she didn't somehow try to find his family. That she didn't seek them out and write to them – to let them know that someone was with him when he died – that he didn't die alone. That someone was there to hold his hand and comfort him. That he didn't die alone.

Maggie imagined herself as she was now, still sitting next to the Finnish boy, her bony hand on his smooth cheek, as if she had never left him, as if she were still giving him comfort.

She looked out at the darkening sky, remembering. The light grew dim. The sounds of the day became hushed and a few crickets began to chirp. Slowly, she stood up from the bench, her joints stiff, and walked into her house.

Mosaic

A little girl in a white ruffled dress, in a room of tearful women, stony-faced elders, and her grief-stricken father. In the coffin lay her mother, Eileen, beautiful dark-haired Eileen. The little girl's only thought as she pulled herself free from her protectors was to crawl into the coffin and be with her mother – then everything would be all right again. They would be together. A piercing scream as they pulled her away, as she fought with her tiny might to be with her mother. Free again, she hid behind her mother's coffin, in the dim corner behind the fern, behind the flowers – crouching, waiting, thinking, I have to be with her.

*

Then, a dream that night and many nights after, of Eileen, of the promise to return. Only wait, my darling child. The harsh prairie winters, wind-blown, bleak. Inside the little girl in her woolens and hand-me-downs was a bright golden spot of her mother's love – and the promise to return. The golden dream, the smile, the promise. Even after the dreams stopped, the golden laughter remained.

*

Run, run. At twelve she could outrun them all. Running to ocean dreams and wings outspread. Almost there. Keep your legs moving. Run and run, farther and farther. Resting at the fence near the flower-filled meadow, and then sitting in the grasses along the twisting creek. She pushed a clump of dirt into the sunset stream, rippling the pink shimmering water. Then she lay back and gazed up at the sky – pink and blue, deep charcoal gray in the distance where a storm brewed. Black streaks of birds crossed the sky and settled on the limbs of bare trees. And she saw it smile and felt it wrap itself around her. The same as her mother's love and embrace. She smiled back at the earth meadow sky, the birds and flowers. Lost mother, eternal mother. She picked the flowers and grasses and carried them home with her. Placed them under her pillow, grass smell enticing her soul at night, the scent of wind and earth and the dying seasons, the tenderness she felt for these changing things that slipped through her fingers as she tried to hold onto them. And in her sleep, fragrance – grass hair, meadow skin, sky eyes. And the smile, the lovely golden smile.

*

Small and beautiful, straight-backed and dark-haired like Eileen. In her nurse's uniform, she posed for the photographer. Her mission: to save the world. She would help the war veterans, the orphans, the sick children. She would be there to hold the hand of the dying soldier, to smooth the brow of the ailing child. To all, her golden smile she would give. And with that faraway determined dream in her eyes, the photographer snapped – and froze that golden radiance forever. Soft large eyes, full lipsticked lips, white nurse's cap pinned to her dark curls. Strike out now on your own. It is time to help the poor world, to show it the golden laughter and meadow tenderness.

*

The war over. Soldiers, now home and grown into men. Soldiers, just ordinary townsfolk again. Soldiers, once again their mothers' sons, not the freedom-fighting heroes in silver airplanes. Soldiers, with their medals in a box somewhere in a chest of drawers. Soldiers, with tales of war humorous and woeful, told at the small-town tavern. Soldiers, fathers now. Soldiers, married to army nurses. One nurse, with her white cap pinned to her dark curls. One nurse, with a faraway look in her eye. One such nurse, now married to one such soldier, back in his small town, far, far from ocean dreams. Now no meadow to run to, no beach to walk along. Give yourself to this husband and to these children. As Eileen gave herself to hers. As Eileen gave her life. Headstrong Eileen, willful Eileen. Tender, lovely Eileen. With her mother's fire and love, the nurse wife goes on. Days and hours and years of lifting cleaning gathering, she goes on. And into her children passes that golden smile, that embrace of the world.

*

The orphan-nurse-wife-mother gave and gave. And laughed and smiled and took care of her golden-filled children. Took care of the soldier-husband-provider who went to the tavern and came home drunk and pushed aside the food she had warmed for him. That nurse-wife grew flowers, wrote poems, warmed baby bottles, loved her children. She learned to walk at night to see the stars, to smell the grasses around her. She inhaled the star grass air, mingling it with her breath, and breathed star grass air into her home, and her children breathed it, and it entered their dreams.

*

Silent torture. Soul-crumpling pain. Dark fear when he came home late. Hard years. The golden light there somewhere. The children gone their way, to their wishes and wants. Alone with the man who used to be her young soldier. Now, a shell of a disappointed man, who couldn't find his worth in life, who tried to squeeze her worth from her and demanded to know, to have, the golden smile. He squeezed her till she nearly had no star grass meadow breath left in her. When he died, she picked herself up from the earth, where she crouched, trying to catch her breath – to catch her breath, or die.

*

He is gone. The children with the golden light in them are gone. They are adults. They have their own children. It seems a different world now. A bit frightened of it. It doesn't feel familiar. She knows where the stars are, still walks out under the night sky and fills herself with night beauty. But the grass, the meadow, what was it? It evades her, that thought, that memory. What was it all, this broken and pieced-back-together thing called Life?

Child woman. Eileen's child. You are the meadow and the grass scent. You are the flower garden, the photograph of determination, the running child. You are the hard days and the leftover meals and the flapping laundry on the line. You are the shimmering pink stream at sunset and the dream of the ocean and the star breath. You are those children. You are your mother. You are nurse-child-wisewoman-daughter eternal. Mother's love lives in you as it lives in the children you bore. The golden laughter you always laughed ripples through them now – because you loved, and were loved, and still love, and are a part of it all. The golden laughter eternal.

April Glory

The winds were wild the day you died
Pear blossoms scattered like snow.
First green tipped the thin tree branches
And your redbud flowered in purple.
Cold wind and sunshine embraced us
As we crossed from house to house.
And the grass and hedge surrounding your yard
Shone in an emerald green.

I knew you had a hand in it –
Delighting in the April glory.
A day of beauty and laughter
When heaven touched earth in joy.